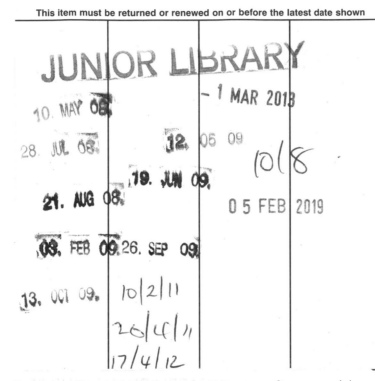

British Library Cataloguing in Publication Data

A catalogue record for this book is
available from the British Library.

ISBN-10: 0340 89354 0
ISBN-13: 978 0340 89354 8

First published in hardback in 2005.
This paperback edition published in 2006.

Published by Hodder Children's Books,
a division of Hachette Children's Books
338 Euston Road, London NW1 3BH

10 9 8 7 6 5 4 3 2

Colour Reproduction by Dot Gradations Ltd, UK
Printed in China

BOKOBIKES

MICK INKPEN

Hodder
Children's
Books

A division of Hachette Children's Books

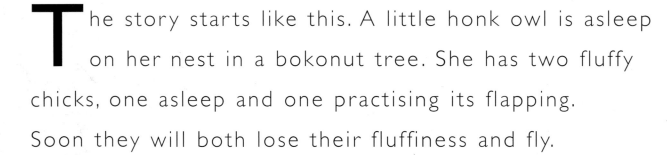

The story starts like this. A little honk owl is asleep on her nest in a bokonut tree. She has two fluffy chicks, one asleep and one practising its flapping. Soon they will both lose their fluffiness and fly.

Down below a squeaking noise.

It is the wheel of Hatz' bike. He is riding slowly round the bokonut tree while Ploo watches.

It is not easy to ride your bike on a sandy beach, and since Ploo and Hatz live on the beach riding their bikes is never as much fun as it should be, especially when Dig gets in the way, which he is doing now.

'You have a go,' says Hatz to Ploo.

But Ploo can't do any better. He struggles once around the bokonut tree with Dig chasing in and out of the pedals.

Then the sand grabs his wheel and steers him into the tree. Bump!

**S**everal things happen at once now.

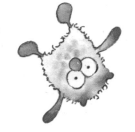Two bokonuts fall out of the tree.

A chick falls out of the nest.

Ploo falls off Hatz' bike.

Dig bites the bicycle tyre.

The bicycle tyre bursts.

A bokonut bounces off Ploo's head.

Another lands in Hatz' hands.

An idea pops into Hatz' head.

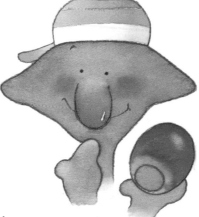

The little chick plops onto the sand.

ig sniffs the little honk owl chick.

'We'll have to climb up and put him back,' says Ploo.

But Hatz is not listening. He is bouncing the bokonut on the sand and catching it. And with each bounce the idea in his head is growing bigger.

Suddenly he tucks the bokonut under his arm, picks up his bike and leaves Blue Nose Beach, without a word.

Ploo balances the little honk owl chick on his head and climbs the bokonut tree.

Very, very gently he tucks it back into the nest, careful not to wake the sleeping birds.

Clunk!

A loud noise from the direction of Hatz' house.

The second little honk owl chick opens an eye. It sees Ploo, gives a frightened little honk, flaps its wings and falls out of the nest. It flutters to the ground and flops onto the sand.

More strange sounds from Hatz' house.

Clink! Clank! Clunk! And a sort of puffing noise.

'I wonder what he's doing,' thinks Ploo.

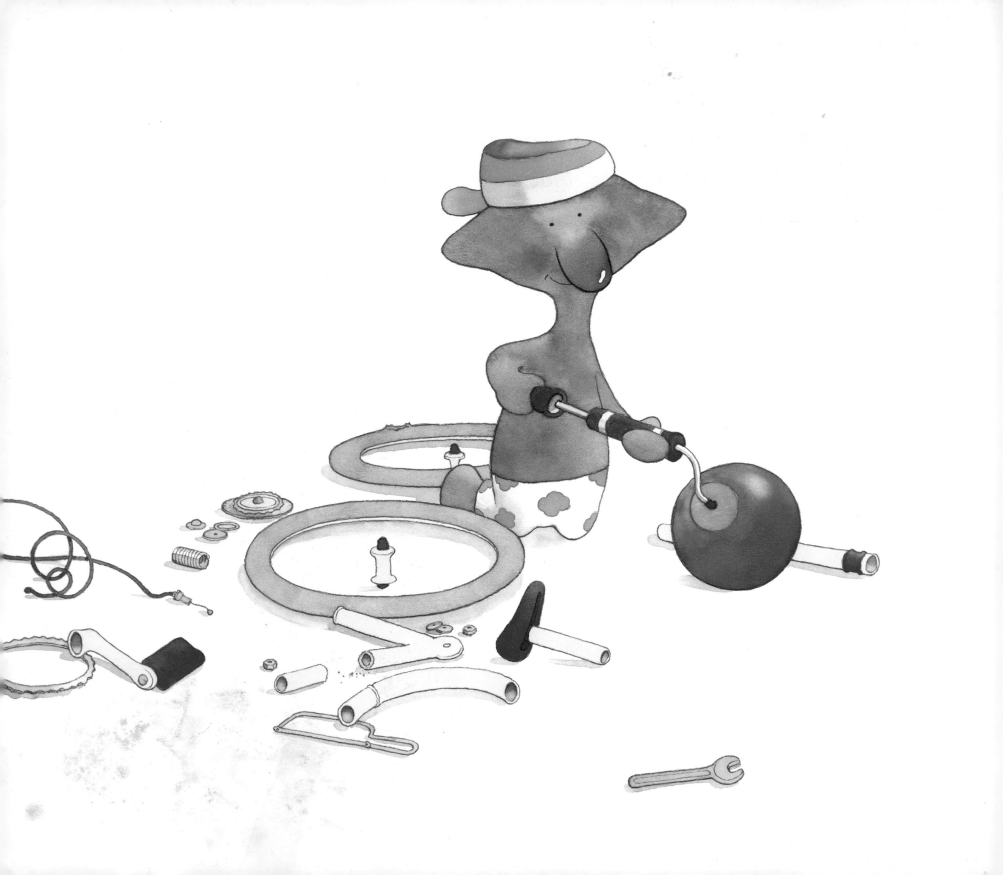

Hatz is surrounded by bits of bike.

Some bits he has undone, some bits he has bent and some bits he has sawn right off!

He is blowing up the bokonut with his pump. With each puff the bokonut grows until it is twice as big as before! Carefully he pulls out the pump. The bokonut makes a small rude noise.

Then nothing. No hissing. No escaping air.

Hatz looks at the hole and is pleased to see that the rubbery stuff inside the bokonut has mended it perfectly!

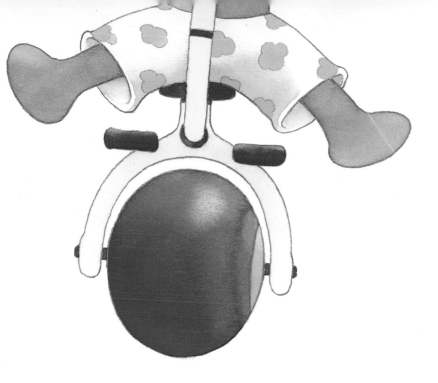

In no time Hatz has finished
his invention.

　Half bike, half bokonut.

　But what is it?

　And what is its name?

　Something made from a
bokonut and a bicycle.

　Something that bounces.
Something that bounces very high!

But what shall we call it?

Ploo is climbing again. He reaches the nest where both birds are sleeping soundly. Carefully he squeezes the little honk owl chick next to its mother. It snuggles down, honks once and straight away its eyes begin to close.

Suddenly, Boing!

Boing!

Boing!

'Look Ploo! Look what I've invented! It doesn't get stuck in the sand!'

H atz is bouncing!
Hatz is almost flying!
Hatz has a really silly grin on his face!
But Hatz is out of control.
One bounce. . .
two bounces. . .
three bounces. . .
He bashes into the bokonut tree!
Down comes the nest!
Down come all the little honk owls!
Down comes Ploo, too!

The little honk owl chicks
flap their fluffy wings.

They fall

and flap

and fall,

and flutter. . .

. . . and for the very first time, they fly!

Away they go, honking little happy honks,
following their mother to the junglywood,
where they will be safe.

But what has happened to Ploo?

Ploo is high in the air, clinging on to
Hatz, who is clinging on to his invention.
They rise and cartwheel slowly.
They arc, then drop and crash onto the sand.
Dig emerges from behind the tree.
The bokonut wheel stops spinning.
Ploo gives it a squeeze.
'You've invented a BOKOBIKE!'
he says.

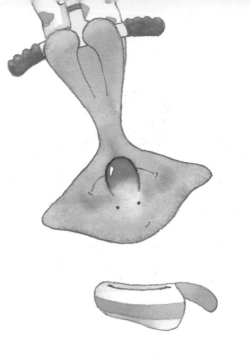

In less than three days they have perfected bokohops, grabbers, sidewinders, backhand jellyrolls, and double boomerloops.

In less than a week Hatz has made another bokobike out of Ploo's old tricycle.

And in less than a fortnight. . .

More Blue Nose Island stories:

Ploo and the Terrible Gnobbler
Beachmoles and Bellvine

Other books by Mick Inkpen:

The Kipper books
The Wibbly Pig books
One Bear at Bedtime
The Blue Balloon
Billy's Beetle
Threadbear
Penguin Small
Lullabyhullaballoo!
Nothing
The Great Pet Sale
Bear